For Jeannie B.
To her, from me.

All Ready

DAVID McKAY COMPANY, INC.

for School

by Leone Adelson

illustrated by
Kathleen Elgin

NEW YORK, PUBLISHERS

This is the day before tomorrow,
and tomorrow is a very important
day for Patty.

Will it rain or will it shine?
Will it be warm or cool?
Rain or shine, come what may,
tomorrow is THE DAY.

Everything is ready.

New shoes . . . .

New socks . . . .

New dress . . . .

And two new hair ribbons to match the dress.

Everything is all ready for tomorrow.

And Patty is all ready for *SCHOOL!*

Patty is full of wanting to go to school. Oh, perhaps there is one tiny spot inside of her that wants to stay home, but Patty scarcely notices it in her excitement. There is too much else to think about — new sights and sounds and feelings, new things to talk about, and new folks to say hello to when school starts.

Oh, will tomorrow never come?

Not that Patty was the only one waiting for tomorrow. Oh no! For the news had spread beyond the house into the garden, beyond the garden into the fields, and beyond the fields into the woods. Soon all the outdoor creatures knew about it.

"Heard the news?" asked one piglet of another.
"Patty's going to school tomorrow."
The second piglet was so taken by surprise
he could only grunt. "Oink," he said.

"Patty's going to school tomorrow,"
a mother blue jay told her children.
"Any worms there?" asked one of the youngsters.

A young rabbit reported the news to his sister.
"Patty's going to school," he said.
"Yum, yum, yum," replied the sister.
"Silly thing," answered the brother. "School
is not to eat."
"No? Then what is it?" the sister asked.
"Who knows?" replied the brother rabbit.

"Patty's going to school," a mother duck quacked over her shoulder.

"Patty's going to school," the first young duck repeated over *his* shoulder.

"Patty's going to school," the second young duck repeated over *his* shoulder.

The third young duck looked over HIS shoulder. There was no one there. "Well," he said, "if school has a muddy bottom AND frogs, why don't we all go?"

And so it was agreed.

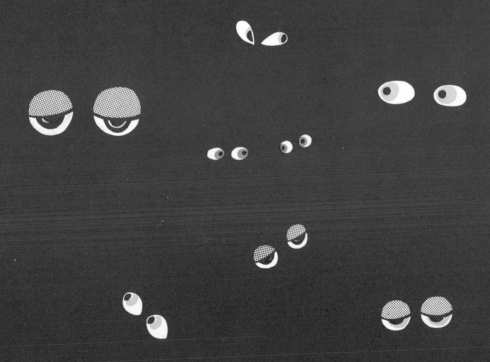

By the time night had fallen every nest,
hive, burrow, glade, barnyard and tree hole
in the neighborhood was bursting with excitement. All the creatures were determined to
follow their friend Patty to school next day
even though it were at the end of the world.
And for all they knew, it was.

Next day Patty left the house clutching
her Daddy's hand tightly in her own. Though
she wanted so much to go to school, suddenly
a tiny part of her — perhaps it was only her
new shoes! — wanted to stay at home.

"I feel a little mixed up," she said,
and her Daddy understood just what she meant.
"It's the feeling of beginning something new,"
he explained. "Grown-ups have it too."
"Even you, Daddy?" Patty exclaimed.
"Even me," Daddy laughed. "Sometimes people
are not too grown up to feel mixed up."
Talking and walking, they did not once look behind.
How could they possibly know they had company?

It was only a wonder that the animals did not
stumble over one another, so closely did they
follow on one another's heels. But they made
no noise — not a quack nor a grunt — and Patty
and her Daddy never knew that behind them came . . .

three young ducks
three rabbits
four blue jays
one fawn
one bright-eyed squirrel

two raccoons
one spiderling whose ninety-nine brothers
and sisters had other things to do
two woodchucks
three pigs — fat ones
and Patty's puppy dog who went everywhere Patty went.

When they arrived at school, Daddy opened
the door and kissed Patty good-by. The
teacher smiled and took Patty's hand. Before
the animals knew what was what, Patty and her
teacher disappeared into the schoolroom.

KINDERGARTEN
CLASS

But the squirrel had come to see what school
was like, and he was not to be outdone, not he!
In a trice he was up a tree and out on a branch.

All the other animals soon found good places
from which they could see what went on.
   "If school is a good place, we'll go too,"
they assured one another.

But they did not dream that what they would see
would surprise them, to say the least.

The pigs opened their little eyes in astonishment
at what Patty was doing.

"Not that way!" they squealed mightily. "You must
roll in it, for mud's sake! Roll in it!"

But Patty was having too good a time to heed them.

Soon the pigs gave up trying to advise her. Curling
their tails tightly they went home in a huff.

"Finger painting!" they sneered. "We pigs will do
as we've always done, and we always will."

And so they did.

The woodchucks whistled a warning.

"You cannot dig with a thing-a-ma-jig!" they cried. "Come back home with us — we'll teach you the right way."

Would Patty listen? No indeed!

So the woodchucks went home in a huff. "Humph," they sniffed, "paws alone are good enough for us. We woodchucks will do as we've always done, and we always will."

And so they did.

The fawn's nose twitched as she watched Patty.
"If she doesn't eat that stuff she hasn't much sense,"
the fawn said, trying to catch Patty's attention.

But Patty was too busy watering the window garden.

"I can't stand watching that good green stuff being
watered instead of eaten," said the fawn, and with a
flick of her tail she bounded off in a huff. "As for
me, I will do as I've always done, and I always will."

And so she did.

The biggest blue jay gave a squawk.

"Why do they just sit there and wait until she OFFERS it to them?" he cried.

"Why aren't they pushing and shoving to be first?" asked another. "*We* did when *we* were little."

"It's really comical to see how little they know about manners," said a third blue jay.

"Come away," said the biggest jay. "I don't want you to watch such goings-on." And he led the youngsters home in a huff. "Mind you do as we've always done and always will," he warned them.

And so they did.

The raccoons were shocked. Pointing their noses earthward, and their tails skyward, they went home in a huff.

"Did you see her eat that cookie without WASHING it first?" they asked one another.

"Hush!" said one of them. "It was unspeakable! We raccoons will do as we've always done, and we always will."

And so they did.

"Very pretty, I *suppose,*" said the eldest rabbit sarcastically, "but entirely wrong from our point of view. Capering should be done at night in the open fields, under a moon."

He thumped his hind leg to get Patty's attention.

"Oh, she won't listen to us," said the youngest rabbit. "She's bewitched, that's what she is."

Twitching their ears furiously, they hopped off in a huff. "School or no school," they said, "we rabbits will do as we've always done, and we always will."

And so they did.

"Spin a thread and dangle," advised the spider. He watched Patty as she traveled the length of the ladder hand over hand. "Foolish girl," he said. "There is an easier way. Look, like this."

He raised his chest, spun a silken thread, kicked himself free, and floated off. Looking down he saw that Patty was climbing the jungle gym.

"Well, if that's all she thinks of me!" thought the spider, floating off in a huff. "I and my ninety-nine brothers and sisters will always keep to the old ways."

And so they did.

Now the teacher took a big picture book from the shelf and read the children a story. The ducks watched.

Suddenly Duck Number One cried out in alarm. "Look!" he quacked. "There are some creatures just like ourselves!"

"But they are squashed flat in that book thing," cried Duck Number Two

"Look! Now she has shut them up tight!" exclaimed Duck Number Three, as the teacher closed the book and put it away.

"Quick, let's get away before she does it to us!" said the first duck, waddling off as fast as he could.

Wagging their tail ends the ducks disappeared.

Only the puppy dog was still waiting when it was time for the children to go home. Patty gave him a little hug and he followed her and one of her new friends to the gate.

"Oh, I think school is just wonderful!" he heard Patty say. His tail wagged as though to say, "Me too."

"I'm coming back tomorrow; aren't you?" Patty's friend asked.

Patty looked amazed. "Why, of course! I'm coming to school every single day."

"Me too," the puppy dog's tail seemed to say.

"Well, so long for now," said Patty's new friend. "Shall I call for you tomorrow morning?"

"Yes, but come early," Patty replied, "because I'll be all ready for school."

And so she was.